"If you start highlighting what stuns you about *Signs Preceding the End of the World*, Yuri Herrera's debut novel in English, every page will be mottled with fluorescent lines. Herrera writes in prose that feels like you are standing on both sides of the uncanny valley while something beautiful happens below and above you, creating a delectable unease, cut through with the simple joy of precise and surprising images. Herrera will draw the obvious comparisons to Roberto Bolaño, but *Signs Preceding the End of World* should also find a home next to Jesse Ball and Italo Calvino."

Josh Cook, Porter Square Books, Boston, MA,
and author of *An Exaggerated Murder*

"Herrera gives us what all great literature should – poetic empathy for dire situations in a life more complex and dynamic than we imagined. And Other Stories gives us what all publishers should – access to this world. I always want more."

Lance Edmonds, Posman Books
(Chelsea Market branch), New York, NY

"Several things occurred while I read *Signs Preceding the End of the World* by Yuri Herrera: I didn't stop talking about it to other book people. When I finished it, I immediately flipped back to the beginning. And then, while waiting for the train, a bird pooped on me. I could go into the beautiful sentences, the structure, or the imagery. But really, a bird pooped on me – right on the shoulder, in the most obvious place – and I didn't even notice until I put the book down."

Jess Marquardt, Greenlight Bookstore, Brooklyn, NY

"A dazzling little thing, containing so much more than the width of its spine should allow. I am in awe-filled love with its heroine: Makina is a vibrantly real presence in a shadowy world of constant threat, her voice perfectly rendered, her unflappable poise tested but never broken."

Gayle Lazda, London Review Bookshop, London

SIGNS PRECEDING
THE END
OF THE WORLD

Yuri Herrera

Translated by
Lisa Dillman

LONDON · NEW YORK

First published in English translation in 2015 by And Other Stories
London – New York
www.andotherstories.org

First published as *Señales que precederán al fin del mundo* in 2009 by
Editorial Periférica, Cáceres, Spain

ISBN 9781908276421
eBook ISBN 9781908276438

Editor: Lorna Scott Fox; Copy-editor: Briony Everroad; Proofreader: Alex
Billington; Typesetter: Tetragon, London; Typefaces: Linotype Swift
Neue and Verlag; Cover Design: Hannah Naughton. The cover image
is reproduced courtesy of Carol M. Highsmith's America, Library of
Congress, Prints and Photographs Division.

A catalogue record for this book is available from the British Library.

SIGNS PRECEDING
THE END OF THE WORLD

For my Grandmother Nina, my Aunt Esther,
and my Uncle Miguel, on their way.

1

THE EARTH

I'm dead, Makina said to herself when everything lurched: a man with a cane was crossing the street, a dull groan suddenly surged through the asphalt, the man stood still as if waiting for someone to repeat the question and then the earth opened up beneath his feet: it swallowed the man, and with him a car and a dog, all the oxygen around and even the screams of passers-by. I'm dead, Makina said to herself, and hardly had she said it than her whole body began to contest that verdict and she flailed her feet frantically backward, each step mere inches from the sinkhole, until the precipice settled into a perfect circle and Makina was saved.

Slippery bitch of a city, she said to herself. Always about to sink back into the cellar.

This was the first time the earth's insanity had affected her. The Little Town was riddled with bullet holes and tunnels bored by five centuries of voracious silver lust, and from time to time some poor soul accidentally discovered just what a half-assed job they'd done of covering them over. A few houses had already been sent packing to the underworld, as had a soccer pitch and half an empty school. These things always happen to someone else, until they happen to you, she thought. She had a quick peek over the precipice, empathized with the poor soul on his way to hell. Happy trails, she said without irony, and then muttered Best be on with my errand.

Her mother, Cora, had called her and said Go and take this paper to your brother. I don't like to send you, child, but who else can I trust it to, a man? Then she hugged her and held her there on her lap, without drama or tears, simply because that's what Cora did: even if you were two steps away it was always as if you were on her lap, snuggled between her brown bosoms, in the shade of her fat, wide neck; she only had to speak to you for you to feel completely safe. And she'd said Go to the Little Town, talk to the top dogs, make nice and they'll lend a hand with the trip.

She had no reason to go see Mr. Double-U first, but a longing for water led her to the steam where he spent his time. She could feel the earth all the way under her nails as though she'd been the one to go down the hole.

The sentry was a proud, sanguine boy who Makina had once shucked. It had happened in the awkward way those things so often do, but since men, all of them, are convinced that they're such straight shooters, and since it was clear that with her he'd misfired, from then on the boy hung his head whenever he ran into her. Makina strolled past him and he came out of his booth as if to say No one gets through, or rather Not you, you're not getting through, but his impulse lasted all of three seconds, because she didn't stop and he didn't dare say any of those things and could only raise his eyes authoritatively once she'd already gone by and was entering the Turkish baths.

Mr. Double-U was a joyful sight to see, all pale roundness furrowed with tiny blue veins; Mr. Double-U stayed in the steam room. The pages of the morning paper were plastered to the tiles and Mr. Double-U peeled them back one by one as he progressed in his reading. He looked at Makina, unsurprised. What's up, he said. Beer? Yeah, Makina said. Mr. Double-U grabbed a beer from a bucket of ice at his feet, popped the top with his hand and passed it to her. They each uptipped the bottle and drank it all down, as if it were a contest. Then in silence they enjoyed the scuffle between the water inside and the water outside.

So how's the old lady? Mr. Double-U inquired.

A long time ago, Cora had helped Mr. Double-U out; Makina didn't know what had happened exactly, just that at the time Mr. Double-U was on the run and Cora had hidden him till the storm blew over. Ever since then, whatever Cora said was law.

Oh, you know. Alive, as she likes to say.

Mr. Double-U nodded, and then Makina added She's sending me on an assignment, and indicated a cardinal point.

Off to the other side? Mr. Double-U asked. Makina nodded yes.

Ok, go, and I'll send word; once you're there my man will get you across.

Who?

He'll know you.

They sat in silence once more. Makina thought she could hear all the water in her body making its way through her skin to the surface. It was nice, and she'd always enjoyed her silences with Mr. Double-U, ever since she first met him back when he was a scared, skinny animal she brought pulque and jerky to while he was in hiding. But she had to go, not just to do what she had to do, but because no matter how tight she was with him, she knew she wasn't allowed to be there. It was one thing to make an exception, and quite another to change the rules. She thanked him,

Mr. Double-U said Don't mention it, child, and she versed.

She knew where to find Mr. Aitch but wasn't sure she'd be able to get in, even though she knew the guy guarding the entrance there, too: a hood whose honeyed words she'd spurned, but she knew what he was like. They said he'd offed a woman, among other things; left her by the side of the road in an oil drum on orders from Mr. Aitch. Makina had asked him if it was true back when he was courting her, and all he said was Who cares if I did or not, what counts is I please 'em all. Like it was funny.

She got to the place. *Pulquería Raskolnikova*, said the sign. Beneath it, the guard. This one she couldn't swish past, so she stopped in front and said Ask him if he'll see me. The guard stared back with glacial hatred and gave a nod, but didn't budge from the door; he stuck a piece of gum in his mouth, chewed it for a while, spat it out. He eyed Makina a little longer. Then turned half-heartedly, as though about to take a leak simply to pass the time, sauntered into the cantina, came back out and leaned against the wall. Still saying nothing. Makina snorted and only then did the guard drawl Are you going in or what?

Inside there were probably no more than five drunks. It was hard to tell for sure, because there was often one facedown in the sawdust. The place smelled, as it should, of piss and fermented fruit. In the back, a curtain separated the scum from the VIPs: though it was just a piece of cloth, no one entered the inner sanctum without permission. I don't have all day, Makina heard Mr. Aitch say.

She pulled the curtain aside and behind it found the bird-print shirt and glimmering gold that was Mr. Aitch playing dominoes with three of his thugs. His thugs all looked alike and none had a name as far as she knew, but not one lacked a gat. Thug .45 was on Mr. Aitch's side playing against the two Thugs .38. Mr. Aitch had three dominoes in his hand and glanced sidelong at Makina without setting them down. He wasn't going to invite her to sit.

You told my brother where to go to settle some business, said Makina. Now I'm off to find him.

Mr. Aitch clenched a fist around the bones and stared straight at her.

You gonna cross? he asked eagerly, though the answer was obvious. Makina said Yes.

Mr. Aitch smiled, sinister, with all the artlessness of a snake disguised as a man coiling around your legs. He shouted something in a tongue Makina didn't speak, and when the barman poked his head around the curtain said Some pulque for the young lady.

The barman's head disappeared and Mr. Aitch said Of course, young lady, of course . . . You're asking for my help, aren't you? Too proud to spell it out but you're asking me for help and I, look at me, I'm saying *Of course*.

Here came the hustle. Mr. Aitch was the type who couldn't see a mule without wanting a ride. Mr. Aitch smiled and smiled, but he was still a reptile in pants. Who knew what the deal was with this heavy and her mother. She knew they weren't speaking, but put it down to his top-dog hubris. Someone had spread that he and Cora were related, someone else that they had a hatchet to bury, though she'd never asked, because if Cora hadn't told her it was for a reason. But Makina could smell the evil in the air. Here came the hustle.

All I ask is that you deliver something for me, an itty bitty little thing, you just give it to a compadre and he'll be the one who tells you how to find your kin.

Mr. Aitch leaned over toward one of the .38 thugs and said something in his ear. The thug got up and versed from the VIP zone.

The barman reappeared with a dandy full of pulque.

I want pecan pulque, Makina said, and I want it cold, take this frothy shit away.

Perhaps she'd gone too far, but some insolence was called for. The barman looked at Mr. Aitch, who nodded, and he went off to get her a fresh cup.

The thug returned with a small packet wrapped in gold cloth, tiny really, just big enough to hold a couple of tamales, and gave it to Mr. Aitch, who took it in both hands.

Just one simple little thing I'm asking you to do, no call to turn chicken, eh?

Makina nodded and took hold of the packet, but Mr. Aitch didn't let go.

Knock back your pulque, he said, pointing to the barman who'd reappeared, glass at the ready. Makina slowly reached out a hand, drank the pecan pulque down to the dregs and felt its sweet earthiness gurgle in her guts.

Cheers, said Mr. Aitch. Only then did he let the bundle go.

You don't lift other people's petticoats.

You don't stop to wonder about other people's business.

You don't decide which messages to deliver and which to let rot.

You are the door, not the one who walks through it.

Those were the rules Makina abided by and that was why she was respected in the Village. She ran the switchboard with the only phone for miles and miles around. It rang, she answered, they asked for so and so, she said I'll go get them, call back in a bit and your person will pick up, or I'll tell you what time you can find them. Sometimes they called from nearby villages and she answered them in native tongue or latin tongue. Sometimes, more and more these days, they called from the North; these were the ones who'd often already forgotten the local lingo, so she responded to them in their own new tongue. Makina spoke all three, and knew how to keep quiet in all three, too.

The last of the top dogs had a restaurant called Casino that only opened at night and the rest of the day was kept clear so the owner, Mr. Q, could read the papers alone at a table in the dining room, which had high ceilings, tall mullioned windows and gleaming floor-boards. With Mr. Q Makina had her own backstory: two years before she'd worked as a messenger during emergency negotiations he and Mr. Aitch held to divvy up the mayoral candidates when their supporters were on the verge of hacking one another to pieces. Midnight messages to a jittery joe who had no hand in the back-room brokering and suddenly, on hearing the words Makina relayed (which she didn't understand, even if she understood), decided to pull out. An envelope slipped to a small-town cacique who went from reticent to diligent after a glance at the contents. Through her, the top dogs assured surrender here and sweet setups there, no bones about it; thus everything was resolved with discreet efficiency.

Mr. Q never resorted to violence – at least there was nobody who'd say he did – and he'd certainly never been heard to raise his voice. Anyhow, Makina had neither been naive nor lost any sleep blaming herself for the invention of politics; carrying messages was her way of having a hand in the world.

Casino was on a second floor, and the door downstairs was unguarded; why bother: who would dare? But Makina had no time to ask for an appointment and anyone who knew her knew she wasn't one to put people out for the sake of it. She'd already arranged for her crossing and how to find her brother, now she had to make sure there would be someone to help her back; she didn't want to stay there, nor have to endure what had happened to a friend who stayed away too long, maybe a day too long or an hour too long, at any rate long enough too long that when he came back it turned out that everything was still the same, but now somehow all different, or everything was similar but not the same: his mother was no longer his mother, his brothers and sisters were no longer his brothers and sisters, they were people with difficult names and improbable mannerisms, as if they'd been copied off an original that no longer existed; even the air, he said, warmed his chest in a different way.

She walked up the stairs, through the mirrored hall and into the room. Mr. Q was dressed, as usual, in black from neck to toe; there were two fans behind him and on the table a national paper, open to the politics. Beside it, a perfect white cup of black coffee. Mr. Q looked her in the eye as soon as Makina versed the mirrored hall, as if he'd been waiting for her, and when she stood before him he made a millimetric move with his head that meant Sit. A few seconds later, without being told, a smocked waiter approached with a cup of coffee for her.

I'm going to the Big Chilango, Makina said; no bush-beating for Mr. Q, no lengthy preambles or kowtows here: even if it seemed that skimming the news was downtime, that was where his world was at work; and she added On a bus, to take care of some family business.

You're going to cross, said Mr. Q. It wasn't a question. Of course not. Forget trying to figure out how he'd heard about it so fast.

You're going to cross, Mr. Q repeated, and this time it sounded like an order. You're going to cross and you're going to get your feet wet and you're going to be up against real roughnecks; you'll get desperate, of course, but you'll see wonders and in the end you'll find your brother, and even if you're sad, you'll wind up where you need to be. Once you arrive, there will be people to take care of everything you require.

He spoke each word very clearly, without stressing any, without moving a single muscle that wasn't strictly necessary. He stopped speaking and took one of Makina's hands, wrapped his fist around it and said This is your heart. Got it?

Mr. Q didn't blink. The light swept the steam from their coffee cups crossways, infusing the air with its bitter scent. Makina thanked him and versed out of there.

She stopped in the mirrored hall to think for a moment about what Mr. Q had said; sometimes she preferred the crass talk of Mr. Aitch, and certainly the slow celebratory tone with which Mr. Double-U spoke; but with Mr. Q nothing went to waste, it was always like pebbles were pouring from his lips, even if she didn't rightly know what each one was supposed to mean.

She looked into the mirrors: in front of her was her back: she looked behind but found only the neverending front, curving forward, as if inviting her to step through its thresholds. If she crossed them all, eventually, after many bends, she'd reach the right place; but it was a place she didn't trust.

2

THE WATER CROSSING

She couldn't get lost. Every time she came to the Big Chilango she trod softly, because that was not the place she wanted to leave her mark, and she told herself repeatedly that she couldn't get lost, and by get lost she meant not a detour or a sidetrack but lost for real, lost forever in the hills of hills cementing the horizon; or lost in the awe of all the living flesh that had built and paid for palaces. That was why she chose to travel underground to the other bus depot. Trains ran around the entire circulatory system but never left the body; down there the heavy air would do her no harm, and she ran no risk of becoming captivated. And she mustn't get lost or captivated, too many people were waiting for her. Someone was covering her post at the switchboard while she was away, but only she spoke all three tongues and only she had mastered the poker face for bad news and the nonchalance with which certain names, oh, so long yearned for, had to be pronounced.

Most important were the ones awaiting her without caring what tongues she spoke or how she couriered. Her kid sister, who'd press close up beside her to eavesdrop on adult troubles, eyes round with attention, hands on knees. Makina could feel her absorbing the world, storing away the passions that came and went along the phone cord. *(Of course I still love you, Very soon, Any day now, Hold your horses, Did you get it? Did she tell you? When was that? How did it happen? How in the name of God is that possible? His name is so and so, Her name is such and such, Don't get me wrong, I never even dreamed, I don't live here anymore.)* She was growing up quickly, and in a man's world, and Makina wanted to educate her as to the essentials: how to take stock of them and how to put up with them; how to savor them. How even if they've got filthy mouths, they're fragile; and even if they're like little boys, they can really get under your skin.

And the boyfriend. A boyfriend she had and who she referred to that way though they'd never discussed it and she didn't feel like anyone's girl, but she called him her boyfriend because he acted so much like a boyfriend that not calling him so, at least to herself, would have been like denying him something written all over his face. A boyfriend. She'd shucked him for the first time back during the brouhaha about the mayors. The day it all ended Makina felt a little like getting wasted, but she didn't so much feel like liquor, it was more an itch to shake her body, so she'd been reckless and gone and shucked him as she had others on a couple of trips to the Little Town; what's more, it had been an entirely forgettable foray. And, no question, she'd shaken off the exhaustion of an ordeal that was now over; but even though she hadn't wanted to be fawned over, just wanted a man to lend himself, he had touched her with such reverence that it must have been smoldering inside him for ages.

She'd seen him before at the door of the elementary school where he worked, had noticed the way he wouldn't look at her, looking instead at every other thing around her; that was where she picked him up, sauntered over saying she needed a shawl so that he'd put his arms round her, took him for a stroll, laughed like a halfwit at everything he said, especially if it wasn't funny, and finally reeled him in on a line she was tugging from her bedroom. The man made love with a feverish surrender, sucked her nipples into new shapes, and when he came was consumed with tremors of sorrowful joy.

After that the man had gone to work in the Big Chilango, and when he came back months later he showed up at the switchboard to tell her something, looking so cocksure and so smart that she guessed what it was that he wanted to say and fixed it so she wouldn't be left alone with him. The man hovered in silence for

Yuri Herrera

hours on end until she said Come back another day, we'll talk. But when he came back she asked him about his gig and about his trip and never about what was going on inside. Then she asked him to stop coming to her work, said she'd seek him out instead. And she did: every weekend they'd shuck, and whenever she sensed he was about to declare himself, Makina would kiss him with extra-dirty lust just to keep his mouth shut. So she'd managed to put off defining things until the eve of the journey she was being sent on by Cora. Then, before she could silence him, he threw up his hands and though he didn't touch her she felt like he was hurling her from the other end of the room.

You're scared of me, he said. Not cause of something I did, just cause you want to be.

He'd stood and was facing her, straightening his sky-blue shirt; he was leaving without making love, but Makina didn't say anything because she saw how hard it had been for him to get up from the bed; she could play dumb – I don't know what you're talking about – or accuse him of making a scene, but the slight tremble betrayed by his lips, the bottled-up breathing of a man barely keeping his composure, inspired in her a respect that she couldn't dismiss; so she said It's not that, and he raised his head to look at her, the whole of him an empty space to be filled by whatever it was that Makina had to say, but she stammered We'll talk when I get back and then . . . Before she was through, he'd nodded as if to say Yeah, yeah, just sticking your tongue in my mouth again, and then turned and versed with the weariness of a man who knows he's being played and can't do a thing about it.

Three years earlier one of Mr. Aitch's thugs had turned up with some papers and told Makina that it said right there that they owned a little piece of land, over on the other side of the river, that a gentleman had left it to them. On the paper was a name that might have belonged to the man who had been her father before he disappeared a long time ago, but Makina took no notice and instead asked Cora what the deal was, what that was all about, and Cora said It's nothing, just Aitch up to his tricks. But in the meantime the thug took Makina's brother out drinking and washed his brain with *neutle* liquor and weasel words and that night her brother came home saying I'm off to claim what's ours. Makina tried to convince him that it was all just talk but he insisted Someone's got to fight for what's ours and I got the balls if you don't. Cora merely looked at him, fed up, and didn't say a word, until she saw him at the door with his rucksack full of odds and ends and said Let him go, let him learn to fend for himself with his own big balls, and he hesitated a moment before he versed, and in the doubt flickering in his eyes you could see he'd spent his whole life there like that, holding back his tears, but before letting them out he turned and versed and only ever came back in the form of two or three short notes he sent a long while later.

Two men ogled her in the bus ticket line, one pushed his face close as he passed and said Lucky's my middle name! He didn't brush against her but he felt her up with his breath, the son of a bitch. Makina wasn't used to that sort of thing. Not that she hadn't experienced it, she just hadn't let herself get used to it. She'd either tell them to fuck right off, or decide not to waste her time on such sad sacks; that's what she decided this time. But not because she was used to it. She bought her ticket and boarded the bus. A couple of minutes later she saw the two men get on. They were hardly more than kids, with their peach fuzz and journey pride. Since they probably had no notion of the way real adventures rough you up, they must've thought they were pretty slick adventurers. They jostled each other down the aisle to their seats, a few rows behind Makina's, but the one who had spoken to her came back and said with a smirk Think this is me, and sat down beside her. Makina made no reply. The bus pulled out; almost immediately Makina felt the first contact, real quick, as if by accident, but she knew that type of accident: the millimetric graze of her elbow prefaced ravenous manhandling. She sharpened her peripheral vision and prepared for what must come, if the idiot decided to persist. He did. Barely bothering to fake it, he dropped his left hand onto his own left leg, languidly letting it sag onto the seat and brush her thigh on the way back up, no harm intended, of course. Makina turned to him, stared into his eyes so he'd know that her next move was no accident, pressed a finger to her lips, shhhh, eh, and with the other hand yanked the middle finger of the hand he'd touched her with almost all the way back to an inch from the top of his wrist; it took her one second. The adventurer fell to his knees in pain, jammed into the tight space between his seat and the one in front, and opened his mouth to scream, but before the order reached his brain Makina had already insisted, finger to lips, shhhh, eh; she let him get used to the idea that a woman had jacked him up and then whispered, leaning close, I don't like being pawed by fucking strangers, if you can believe it.

The boy couldn't, judging by the way his eyes were bulging.

You crossing over to find a gig? Makina asked.

The boy nodded emphatically.

Then you'll need every finger you've got, won't you? Cause you can't cook or pick with your tootsies, now, can you?

The boy shook his head no less emphatically.

So, Makina continued. Listen up, I'm going to let you go and you're going to curl up with your little friend back there, and I swear on all your pain that if you even so much as think about me again, the only thing that hand's going to be good for is wiping ass.

The boy opened his mouth but now it was Makina who shook her head.

You believe me? she asked, and as she did so pressed his finger a little farther back. You don't believe me. You believe me?

Something in the boy's tears told Makina he believed her. She released him and watched as he staggered back to his seat. She heard him sniveling for a while and his friend going Holy shit, holy shit, holy shit, over and over; in the meantime she let herself be lulled by the sight of the gray city fleeing past in the opposite direction.

It was nighttime when she awoke. The boy's whimpering had stopped; all you could hear was the engine of the bus and the snoring of passengers. Makina could never be sure of what she'd dreamed, in the same way that she couldn't be sure a place was where the map said it was until she'd gotten there, but she had the feeling she'd dreamed of lost cities: literally, lost cities inside other lost cities, all ambulating over an impenetrable surface.

She looked out at the country mushrooming on the other side of the glass. She knew what it contained, its colors, the penury and the opulence, hazy memories of a less cynical time, villages emptied of men. But on contemplating the tense stillness of the night, the darkness dotted here and there with sparks, on sensing that insidious silence, she wondered, vaguely, what the hell might be festering out there: what grows and what rots when you're looking the other way. What's going to appear? she whispered to herself, pretending that as soon as they passed that lamppost, or that one, or that one, she'd see what it was that had been going on in the shadows. Maybe a whole slew of new things, maybe even some good things; or maybe not. Not even in make-believe did she get her hopes up too high.

The youngsters kept their distance the remainder of the trip. When the bus stopped at gas stations they waited for Makina to get off first and then cautiously emerged, like fugitives, and returned to their seats before she did. They crossed the entire country without one comment on the view.

Finally the bus reached the end of the land, at almost midnight the following day. A string of hotels facing the river was doing well off the mass exodus. Makina cruised around wondering how she'd find Mr. Double-U's contact, but couldn't discern any glance of recognition so decided to go into one of the hotels. She asked for a bed, paid, and they pointed to a door on the first floor but gave her no key. On entering she saw why. It was a very sizeable room with fifteen or twenty bunks on which were piled people of many tongues: girls, families, old folks, and, more than anything else, lone men, some of them still just boys. She closed the door and looked for a space in another room, but found them all equally overcrowded.

She asked for the bathroom. There were just two per floor, one for women and one for men. She went into the women's to take the shower she'd been needing the whole long road from the Big Chilango. She'd barely been able to take birdbaths at the gas stations. She'd scrubbed her armpits, neck, and face, taken off her pants to shake them out. Once she was almost left behind because she took so long drying herself at the hand dryer. Now she could finally wash all over, and didn't mind that there was no hot water in the hotel shower; it was the same in her hometown. As she was soaping herself she heard someone else come into the bathroom, heard the same someone take two steps and stop, heard them deliberating and heard their hands dip into Makina's rucksack and rootle through her things. She poked her head out. It was a woman in her second youth; she looked tired. She had Makina's lipstick in one hand and started to apply it and didn't stop despite the fact that Makina was watching her and the woman could see she was. She watched her gussy up. She did it slowly and confidently, slid the stick from one side to the other of each lip and then swooped it up as if she'd come to the edge of a cliff, smacked her lips together to even out the color, puckered them for an air kiss. When she was done, still staring into the mirror, the woman said Me? I tell you, I'm gonna start off on the right foot; don't know if makeup will help but at least no one can say I showed up scruffy, you know? And only then did she turn to look at Makina. You look very pretty, Makina said. It'll all go great, you'll see. The woman smiled, said Thanks, hon, put the lipstick back and versed.

After her shower she went back to wandering the rooms where those in flight sweated out the night. Many were sleeplessly waiting for their contact to show and tell them it was time. She deciphered a letter for a very old man who couldn't read, in which his son explained how to find him once he'd crossed. She taught a boy how to say Soap in anglo and explained to another that, as far as she'd been told, you weren't allowed to cook on the sidewalk over there. There were traders, too, who'd just crossed back the other way and slept with their arms around bundles of clothes or toys they'd brought to sell.

She versed to the street. Small groups walked the length of the line, moving farther from the glimmer of the northern city till they found their point of departure. Among them she saw the two boys from the bus negotiating the price of crossing with a couple of men. The men retreated a moment to consult together, talking anglo so the others wouldn't understand. Should we just take 'em? asked the first, and the other said Let 'em wait, too bad if they're in a hurry, Plus, word is that security is tight, For real? For real, Damn, then we really should take 'em, or act like we are: got another little group'll pay us more if we cross 'em right now, Let's put these scrubs out as bait and get the others over, Just what I was thinking. That's what they said, in anglo tongue, and Makina heard it as she sidled up and past them. She kept on going and when she got to where the boys were said Watch it, without turning toward them. The one who had touched her flinched, but the other seemed to realize that Makina was talking about something else, not about what a badass she was. Watch it, they're out to screw you; I was you I'd find someone else, she said and kept on. The youngsters looked at the men, the men guessed Makina had said something, both parties swiftly saw the deal was off, and the men went to find new clients.

She walked up and down along the riverbank until the night waned; then she sat at the water's edge to scan the horizon as she ate one last hunk of brittle, sweet and thick with peanut salt, and just as the sun began to rise she saw a light flicker meaningfully on the other side. Against the clear dawn glow she made out a man and saw that she was the one he was signaling to, so she raised an arm and waved it from side to side. The man switched off his light and went to get something from a truck parked a few feet away. He came back with an enormous inner tube, like from a tractor, tossed it into the water, climbed inside and began to cross the river, propelling himself forward with a tiny oar he'd brought along. As he made his way across, Makina could begin to distinguish the features of the silhouetted man: his skin had the dark polish of long hours spent in the sun, a short salt-and-pepper beard softened his face, in the center of which a large nose, slightly hooked, jutted out; he wore a white shirt darkened by the water scaling his torso, and he carried his own rucksack. Though he gave the impression of being short, as soon as he emerged from the river she saw that he was at least two hands taller than her. And wiry. Every muscle in his arms and neck seemed trained for something specific, something strenuous.

Hey there, he said as soon as he was out of the water. So you're going over for a lil land, I hear.

Ha, said Makina, land's the one thing we got enough of. I'm going for my bro, he's the stupid sap who went over for a little land.

Chucho, said the man, holding out a hand.

Makina, she reciprocated. The man's skin was weather-beaten but pleasing to the touch, warm even though he'd only just versed from the water.

Chucho took a pack of cigarettes from his bag, lit two and gave one to Makina. She inhaled deeply, held the smoke in her lungs – in her head she could see it spiraling gaily – and exhaled.

How'd you recognize me? she asked.

They sent me a picture, full body shot.

For a moment Makina thought he'd make some comment about her looks: You're even cuter in the flesh, or What a tasty surprise, or A sight for sore eyes, or any of that oafishness that makes men feel they're being original, but Chucho just kept smoking, face to the dawn.

Wouldn't it be better to wait till it's dark again? she said. Wouldn't it be too easy for them to spot us now?

Nah, they're tied up somewhere else, he said, winked at her and added I got my contacts.

They finished their smokes and then he said Alright, we're off. He pulled another small oar from his pack and handed it to Makina, pushed the tube back in the water and helped Makina get in in front of him.

The first few feet were easy. Makina could still touch bottom and felt his legs tangle with hers as they advanced; she even, before things got rough, felt him lean in close and sniff her hair, and she was glad she'd had the chance to shower. But suddenly the riverbed ducked away and an icy current began to push their feet away like a living thing, relentless. Row, Chucho said; Makina already was but the tube was being tugged into the current as though adrift. Row, repeated Chucho, this is going to be a bitch. Hardly had he spoken when a torrent of water bounced them out, flipping the tube. Suddenly the world turned cold and green and filled with invisible water monsters dragging her away from the rubber raft; she tried to swim, kicking at whatever was holding her but couldn't figure out which side was up or where Chucho had gone. She didn't know how long she struggled frantically, and then the panic subsided, and she intuited that it made no difference which way she headed or how fast she went, that in the end she'd wind up where she needed to be. She smiled. She felt herself smile. That was when the sound of breaking water replaced the green silence. Chucho dragged her out by the pants with both hands: they'd reached the opposite bank and the inner tube was swirling away in the current as if it had urgent business to attend to.

They lay on the shore, spent and panting. It had hardly been more than a few dozen yards, but on staring up at the sky Makina thought that it was already different, more distant or less blue. Chucho stood, scanned the city at their backs and said Well, now, next part's easier.

3

THE PLACE WHERE THE HILLS MEET

First there was nothing. Nothing but a frayed strip of cement over the white earth. Then she made out two mountains colliding in the back of beyond: like they'd come from who knows where and were headed to anyone's guess but had come together at that intense point in the nothingness and insisted on crashing noisily against each other, though the oblivious might think they simply stood there in silence. Yond them hills is the pickup, take you on your way, said Chucho, but we'll make a stop first so you can change.

Then off in the distance she glimpsed a tree and beneath the tree a pregnant woman. She saw her belly before her legs or her face or her hair and saw she was resting there in the shade of the tree. And she thought, if that was any sort of omen it was a good one: a country where a woman with child walking through the desert just lies right down to let her baby grow, unconcerned about anything else. But as they approached she discerned the features of this person, who was no woman, nor was that belly full with child: it was some poor wretch swollen with putrefaction, his eyes and tongue pecked out by buzzards. Makina turned to look at Chucho and see if he too had been fooled, but he hadn't. Chucho told her about how one time he was taking a man back the other way because his wife was dying and they'd gotten lost – this was when he'd only just started crossing folks – and some sonofabitch rancher thought they were headed this direction and it was only because he chased them that they found the way back, but by then it was too late. Cat made it home, Chucho said, but by the time he got there she was already six feet under.

One of the first to strike it rich after going north came back to the Village all full of himself, all la-di-da, all fancy clothes and watches and new words he'd be able to say into his new phone. He made sure to round up every wide-eyed hick he could find, brought each and every one to the switchboard where he planned to teach Makina a lesson in public, as if one time she'd fucked him over, though he claimed he just wanted to show her because she knew about this stuff. He took out two cellphones and gave one to his mother, Here, jefecita, just press this button when you hear the briiiiiiiing and you'll see, just step right outside, and he brandished the other one. He gave Makina two patronizing pats on the forearm and said Tough luck, kid, it had to happen: you're going to be out of a job. Watch and learn. The young man pushed a little key and waited for the zzzz of the dial tone, but the zzzz didn't come. Never mind, no sweat, he said. These new ones don't do that. And proceeded to dial the number of the cellphone his mother was holding to her ear on the other side of the wall. Now at least you could hear peep-peep-peep as he pressed each key, and the wide-eyed stood like ninnies waiting for the thing that they were expecting to happen and yet wishing that it would turn out to be, well, more spectacular somehow, more weird. But the peep-peeps were followed only by silence, a silence that was especially weighty because it seemed as if everyone was holding their breath so as not to spoil the wondrous trick. And the mother was still standing outside, in truth far less concerned about whatever it was her son was up to than about the pot she'd left on the stove, and though the phone was still clamped to her ear she was in fact already telling a neighbor Be an angel, would you? Go check on my stew. And on it went till the guy was left just looking at his phone with all his might, as though enough staring might somehow fix it. Makina held off a bit then said Maybe you should have bought a few cell towers, too? The poor guy turned red when the penny dropped and suddenly he was the only wide-eyed one in the place. That was what Makina said but then she felt mean for messing with him so she gave him a kiss on the cheek and said Don't worry, kid, they'll get here one day.

Before they reached the shack where she was to change clothes, what happened was:

that another truck pulled right up beside them on the road to the mountains; it was black with four searchlights mounted on the roof and the driver was an anglo with dark glasses and a hat with a silver buckle. His eyes shot bullets through the two windows between them, still stepping on it, still stuck to them like glue;

and that Chucho grabbed a cell and started to dial a number but didn't finish till they'd reached the shack, in the foothills, and then dialed the rest when he got out and as soon as they picked up said, in anglo tongue, Hey officer, I got the info I promised, yeah, yeah, right where I said last time, yeah, but be careful, he's armed to the eyeballs, and hung up.

The anglo had pulled up ahead and parked a few yards from the shack. He stood by his truck, fingering the grip of a handgun tucked into his waistband. As soon as they went inside Chucho said Gotta be quick, no telling what we're in for now, best leave behind anything might weigh you down. In the shack all there was

was a cot and a stove, and on the cot a pair of pants, a t-shirt with an anglo print, and a denim jacket; on the stove, a pot of scalded water. Makina began to undress with her back to Chucho, who stood smoking and staring out the window at the goon on guard outside, and thought how strange it was not to feel scared or angry at having to strip naked with no wall to separate them. She took off her blouse. She could have put on the t-shirt before taking off her pants but she didn't. She took off her pants. She took off her bra and panties, too, though Chucho hadn't told her to, and stood there, looking down at the clothes spread out on the cot, with something almost like an urge to pee and something almost like a bated breath tingling up and down her body. Quick, Chucho insisted; Makina knew he was still staring out the window but his voice enveloped her. She felt that moment of tension without fear go on and on, and then was surprised how much time had passed without her feeling guilty for wanting what she wanted. More than leaving her boyfriend behind she was casting off her guilt the way you might shed belongings. But even those interminable seconds came to an end. She said ok, got dressed. Chucho turned around.

What did you say to that person on the phone? she asked.

Just what I reckon, he said, jerking his head toward outside. Like not only is our rancher here a patriot but he's got his own lil undercover business, like it's not so much he's bothered bout us not having papers as he is bout us muscling in on his act.

You sure?

Chucho shrugged. Maybe the dumbfuck is just in up to his neck.

They stood there a moment, Makina staring at him, Chucho absorbed in his thoughts, one eye on the window the whole time. Then he said Well, whatever's going down, time for it to go down, so if the shit hits the fan you head for that mountain pass and stay on the trail, keep the sun on your back.

She waited for him to start for the door before she took from her rucksack a plastic bag with the note Cora had given her and the package Mr. Aitch had entrusted to her and slipped them into her jacket, and then she went after him. Soon as they versed the rancher approached, revolver in hand, though not pointing it at them.

You just took your last trip, coyote.

I'm no coyote, Chucho said.

Ha! I seen you crossing folks, the man said. And looks like now I caught you in the act.

Not the act I'm denying, said Chucho, tho I'm no coyote.

The anglo's expression indicated that he was engaged in a mighty struggle with the nuances of the concept. He scanned Chucho's face for a few seconds, waiting for clarification. And now, yessir, chose to point the gun at them.

What I'm denying, Chucho went on, Is that you caught us.

Then they all registered the fact they had company. Two police trucks were haring across the open country, top speed but no flashing lights. The minute the rancher was distracted by turning to look, Chucho pounced and grabbed the arm that was holding the gun. The rancher shot to kill but it was a waste of bullets since Chucho had wrestled the muzzle away from the two spots where there were bodies. The rancher was big and strong but all his strength was not enough to regain his balance. In the end Chucho stuck one foot between his two and they both fell to the sand. The police trucks had stopped a dozen yards away and the cops inside took aim from behind the open doors.

Git! said Chucho. Makina moved toward him because even though she knew he was talking to her she thought he was asking her for help. He must be asking for help. Makina wasn't used to having people say Run away.

One more bullet exploded from the revolver; Makina saw the barrel head-on, saw the way it dilated the split second it spat fire and the way it contracted just as the bullet clipped her side. The impact caused her to whirl but not fall, and as she span she took two steps forward and dealt the rancher a kick in the jaw. He was still moving but had lost his sense of direction: he was aiming, like his bullets, for Chucho's neck but where he clawed, all there was was air. Chucho punched him in the chin, which didn't knock the man out but did curb his momentum, and said, stressing each word, I can take care of this. Makina looked to the trucks, then again to the men on the sand, then to the mountains, colliding endlessly before her, and started to run, guns and evil bastards on both sides. She heard them behind her, ordering Freeze, on the ground, but didn't turn, not even when she heard another shot that must have come from a police gun because it sounded different, less powerful than the rancher's.

She ran uphill till she could no longer hear shouting behind her, then she turned to look. The cops had the two men in their sights, Chucho's hands on the back of his head and the rancher seemingly unconscious. Another cop looked in Makina's direction but showed no sign of following. Only then did Makina inspect her side. The bullet had entered and versed between two ribs, ignoring her lung, as if it had simply skimmed beneath the surface of her skin so as not to get stuck in her body. She could see the gash of the bullet's path, but it didn't hurt and barely bled. She looked once more to where the men were arguing. Now there was no cop watching her. Chucho was on the ground talking; they stood listening in a semicircle around him. The rancher was still face down.

Makina remembered Chucho's mouth saying I can take care of this. She guessed that he was talking, more than anything, about her, and decided to keep on climbing.

Rucksacks. What do people whose life stops here take with them? Makina could see their rucksacks crammed with time. Amulets, letters, sometimes a *huapango* violin, sometimes a *jaranera* harp. Jackets. People who left took jackets because they'd been told that if there was one thing they could be sure of over there, it was the freezing cold, even if it was desert all the way. They hid what little money they had in their underwear and stuck a knife in their back pocket. Photos, photos, photos. They carried photos like promises but by the time they came back they were in tatters.

In hers, as soon as she'd agreed to go get the kid for Cora, she packed:

a small blue metal flashlight, for the darkness she might encounter,

one white blouse and one with colorful embroidery, in case she came across any parties, three pairs of panties so she'd always have a clean one even if it took a while to find a washhouse,

a latin–anglo dictionary (those things were by old men and for old men, outdated the second they left the press, true, but they still helped, like people who don't really know where a street is and yet point you in the right direction),

a picture her little sister had drawn in fat, round strokes that featured herself, Makina and Cora in ascending order, left to right and short to tall,

a bar of *xithé* soap,

a lipstick that was more long-lasting than it was dark and,

as provisions: amaranth cakes and peanut brittle.

She was coming right back, that's why that was all she took.

4

THE OBSIDIAN MOUND

When she reached the top of the saddle between the two mountains it began to snow. Makina had never seen snow before and the first thing that struck her as she stopped to watch the weightless crystals raining down was that something was burning. One came to perch on her eyelashes; it looked like a stack of crosses or the map of a palace, a solid and intricate marvel at any rate, and when it dissolved a few seconds later she wondered how it was that some things in the world – some countries, some people – could seem eternal when everything was actually like that miniature ice palace: one-of-a-kind, precious, fragile. She felt a sudden stab of disappointment but also a slight subsiding of the fear that had been building since she'd versed from home.

On the other side of the mountains was the truck Chucho had told her about. She went up to it, opened the passenger door and said Are you Aitch's man? The driver jumped out of his skin then tried to recover his hard-boiled slouch, upped his nose as if to say S'right, and finally jerked his head to signal Get in.

On the way the driver turned to look at her every little while, as though hoping she'd try to talk to him so he could refuse, but Makina had no interest in the challenge; she should have been exhausted but what she felt was an overwhelming impatience. She turned to the window to look out without seeing. If she didn't get back soon, what would become of all those people who had no way of communicating with their kith and kin? She had to get back, because Cora was counting on her; and what about the switchboard, how would it look and feel without her? Ay, the guilt, reducing reality to a clenched fist with set hours.

The city was an edgy arrangement of cement particles and yellow paint. Signs prohibiting things thronged the streets, leading citizens to see themselves as ever protected, safe, friendly, innocent, proud, and intermittently bewildered, blithe, and buoyant; salt of the only earth worth knowing. They flourished in supermarkets, cornucopias where you could have more than everyone else or something different or a newer brand or a loaf of bread a little bigger than everyone else's. Makina just dented cans and sniffed bottles and thought it best to verse, and it was when she saw the anglogaggle at the self-checkouts that she noticed how miserable they looked in front of those little digital screens, and the way they nearly-nearly jumped every time the machine went bleep! at each item. And how on versing out to the street they sought to make amends for their momentary one-up by becoming wooden again so as not to offend anyone.

Out on the concrete and steel-girder plain, though, she sensed another presence straight off, scattered about like bolts fallen from a window: on street corners, on scaffolding, on sidewalks; fleeting looks of recognition quickly concealed and then evasive. These were her compatriots, her homegrown, armed with work: builders, florists, loaders, drivers; playing it sly so as not to let on to any shared objective, and instead just, just, just: just there to take orders. They were the same as back home but with less whistling, and no begging.

She was seduced by something less clear-cut as she wandered by the restaurants: unfamiliar sweetness and spiciness, concoctions that had never before passed her lips or her nose, rapturous fried feasts. Places serving food that was strange but with something familiar mixed in, something recognizable in the way the dishes were finished off. So she visited the restaurants, too, with the brevity imposed by glaring managers who guessed She's not here to eat, and it wasn't until the fourth restaurant that she realized they were here, too, more armed than anyplace else, cooks and helpers and dishwashers, ruling the food at the farthest outposts.

All cooking is Mexican cooking, she said to herself. And then she said Ha. It wasn't true, but she liked saying it just the same.

The driver jerked up his palms when he saw Makina take out the package from Mr. Aitch. You don't give nothing to me. Didn't you know that? He dropped her on a deserted street and said Here's where they'll tell you where to take it. Since there was nobody around she ambled through a supermarket and sniffed restaurants. When she returned, a flower store had opened; an old man was sitting at the entrance, resting one hand on a cane and bringing a piece of bread to his mouth with the other. Makina planted herself in front of him. They looked at each other. Again Makina made as if to take the packet out but the old man said Wait, go clean up first and then I'll take you. With his cane he pointed to a little door at the back of the store. Makina went through it, washed her hands and face; the wound on her ribs was dry and when she rubbed the soap across it hardly even stung. When she versed from the bathroom the old man was standing up. Come with me, he said. See those men? Makina saw two guys in a black ride with silver rims. Cops, wondering who you are, he went on. We're going to walk till they get sidetracked. They began walking. The car followed close behind, suddenly accelerated and disappeared, but soon returned to follow them at a distance.

I'm taking you to the stadium, the old man said. If they stop trailing us, you hand it over there; meantime I'll tell you about your kin.

Makina was overcome by foreboding. Is he dead?

No, no, alive and kicking like a mule, he's fine; you'll find him changed, but still, he got here ok. Like you, he brought a little something from Mr. Aitch and things got rough, but then he went off on his business.

Do you know where?

The old man said Help me walk. Makina took his arm and the old man smoothly slipped her a piece of paper with his other hand. Address's right here.

They kept walking. The black car slowed beside them, the occupants eyeballed for a few seconds and took off.

Think it's safe? Makina asked.

Don't know, but it's got to be done.

The stadium loomed before them. So, what do they use that for?

They play, said the old man. Every week the anglos play a game to celebrate who they are. He stopped, raised his cane and fanned the air. One of them whacks it, then sets off like it was a trip around the world, to every one of the bases out there, you know the anglos have bases all over the world, right? Well the one who whacked it runs from one to the next while the others keep taking swings to distract their enemies, and if he doesn't get caught he makes it home and his people welcome him with open arms and cheering.

Do you like it?

Tsk, me, I'm just passing through.

How long you been here?

Going on fifty years . . . Here we are.

They were standing at one of the doors to the stadium. The old man gave a whistle, the door opened, the old man said Get it over with, and turned away.

The darkest kid Makina had ever seen in her life pointed to a corridor. She walked down it toward the light. At the end she was instantly overcome by the sight of a vast expanse, two rival visions of beauty: the bottom an immense green diamond rippling in its own reflection; and above, embracing it, tens of thousands of folded black chairs, an obsidian mound barbed with flint, sharp and glimmering.

She was standing there, dazzled, when from other tunnels around her more men emerged, ten or fifteen or thirty all at once, all black but some blacker than others, some sinewy as if they'd grown up in mountain air, others puffy like aquatic animals, many bald but a few with long matted hair down to their waists. All looking at her and walking toward her, calm and cool but with faces that clearly conveyed they were serious motherfuckers.

Don't let my associates scare you, she suddenly heard behind her, in latin tongue. They're not such tough sonsofbitches, just had to learn to look like it.

Down the corridor she'd walked, a man limped nearer, his features becoming clearer as he was gradually bathed in light: his blazing blond hair was streaked with orange highlights, he held a cigar in one hand and wore mirrored shades. Makina had never laid eyes on him before but there was no mistaking who he was. Mr. P, the fourth top dog, had fled the Little Town after a turf war with Mr. Aitch and every once in a while you'd hear how one way or another they were goading each other from afar. What had Makina gotten herself into? Did Mr. P think he could mess with Mr. Aitch by messing with her?

You got nothing to fear from me neither, girl, said Mr. P, suspecting her guts were churning. And not because Aitch and I have made peace. We do business, sure, but who says that's not just another way to eat the dish cold?

Makina noticed that from his belt hung a long, thin knife and that Mr. P patted it nonstop. Very slowly, she at last pulled out the packet that was for him. Mr. P held out his hand, weighed up the package without taking his eyes off her, and passed it to one of his associates. He patted and patted his knife and smiled at Makina while the associates opened the package, closed the package and in anglo said We're cool. Mr. P, though, kept leering and smiling at Makina and patting his dangling knife, and she wanted to go now but couldn't muster enough of a voice for even the first syllable.

Wouldn't you like to come work for me, child? asked Mr. P, eyeing her crotch.

I'm here for my brother.

Of course, the brother.

Mr. P stopped looking, scratched his chin and repeated The brother, the brother.

His eyes scanned the stadium with idle curiosity, he turned, and the associates began to verse leisurely down the tunnels, until Makina was all alone.

5

THE PLACE WHERE THE WIND
CUTS LIKE A KNIFE

They are homegrown and they are anglo and both things with rabid intensity; with restrained fervor they can be the meekest and at the same time the most querulous of citizens, albeit grumbling under their breath. Their gestures and tastes reveal both ancient memory and the wonderment of a new people. And then they speak. They speak an intermediary tongue that Makina instantly warms to because it's like her: malleable, erasable, permeable; a hinge pivoting between two like but distant souls, and then two more, and then two more, never exactly the same ones; something that serves as a link.

More than the midpoint between homegrown and anglo their tongue is a nebulous territory between what is dying out and what is not yet born. But not a hecatomb. Makina senses in their tongue not a sudden absence but a shrewd metamorphosis, a self-defensive shift. They might be talking in perfect latin tongue and without warning begin to talk in perfect anglo tongue and keep it up like that, alternating between a thing that believes itself to be perfect and a thing that believes itself to be perfect, morphing back and forth between two beasts until out of carelessness or clear intent they suddenly stop switching tongues and start speaking that other one. In it brims nostalgia for the land they left or never knew when they use the words with which they name objects; while actions are alluded to with an anglo verb conjugated latin-style, pinning on a sonorous tail from back there.

Using in one tongue the word for a thing in the other makes the attributes of both resound: if you say Give me fire when they say Give me a light, what is not to be learned about fire, light and the act of giving? It's not another way of saying things: these are new things. The world happening anew, Makina realizes: promising other things, signifying other things, producing different objects. Who knows if they'll last, who knows if these names will be adopted by all, she thinks, but there they are, doing their damnedest.

The paper the old man had slipped her bore an address in another city but it seemed there was no need to verse this one to get to that one: it was simply a matter of riding busses and crossing streets and passing malls and after lots of the first and even more of the second and several of the third, she'd arrive.

She almost didn't realize when she reached it, because the cities had no center for avenues to radiate from. She just suddenly started seeing the name of the other place on stores and fire trucks. She kept walking the way she'd been told by some homegrown anglos she'd spoken to, and as she made her way the sky got redder and the air began to ice up.

Her lips were split and her palms cracked if she pulled them from her jacket pockets.

Eight times she asked before she found the spot and every time the abject answer turned out to be some bleak tundra where they sent her to another bleak tundra:

She asked the way to the city and they told her Over there (finger pointing to where the sun comes up).

She asked farther on for the way to the suburb and they told her There's four with that name, but maybe she wanted the one by the bridge.

She asked farther on for the way to the bridge, but they told her she didn't want that suburb but the one with the zoo.

She asked farther on for the way to the zoo and they told her it was near the statue of a man in a frock coat.

She asked farther on for the way to the statue of

the man in a frock coat and they said Can't you see, it's right behind you.

Then she asked for the way to the street written down and they said This is it.

She asked for the way to her brother, perhaps too urgently, and they shrugged.

She asked finally for the way to the promised land and that person looked annoyed before responding.

There was still some light in the sky but it was turning dark, like a giant pool of drying blood.

Her brother had sent two or three messages back with assorted migrants on their way home. Two or three and not two, or three; Makina couldn't say for sure because after the first one the one that followed and maybe one more were the same old story.

The first one said:

I haven't found the land yet, but it won't be long now, you'll see.

Everything's so stiff here, it's all numbered and people look you in the eye but they don't say anything when they do.

They celebrate here, too, but they don't dance or pray, it's not in honor of anyone. The only real big celebration is the turkey feast, which is a good one because all you do is eat and eat.

It's really lonely here, but there's lots of stuff. I'm going to bring you some when I come. I just have to take care of this and then I'll be back, you'll see.

The second one didn't mention the country or the land or his plans. It said:

I'm fine, I have a job now.

And the third, if it existed, might've made the same claim, this way:

I said I was fine so stop asking.

It had taken everything she had just to pronounce the eight tundras. To cleave her way through the cold on her own, sustained by nothing but an ember inside; to go from one street to another without seeing a difference; to encounter barricades that held people back for the benefit of cars. Or to encounter people who spoke none of the tongues she knew: whole barrios of clans from other frontiers, who questioned her with words that seemed traced in the air. The weariness she felt at the monuments of another history. The disdain, the suspicious looks. And again the cold, getting colder, burrowing into her with insolence.

And when she arrived and saw what she'd come to find it was sheer emptiness.

And yet machines were still at work. That was the first thing she noticed when they pointed the place out to her: excavators obstinately scratching the soil as if they needed urgently to empty the earth; but the breadth of that abyss and the clean cut of its walls didn't correspond to the modest exertion of the machines. Whatever once was there had been pulled out by the roots, expelled from this world; it no longer existed.

I don't know what they told you, declared the irritated anglo, I don't know what you think you lost but you ain't going to find it here, there was nothing here to begin with.

6

THE PLACE WHERE FLAGS WAVE

Scum, she heard as she climbed the eighth hill from which, she was sure, she'd catch sight of her brother. You lookin to get what you deserve, you scum? She opened her eyes. A huge redheaded anglo who stank of tobacco was staring at her. Makina knew the bastard was just itching to kick her or fuck her and got slowly to her feet without taking her eyes off him, because when you turn your back in fear is when you're at the greatest risk of getting your ass kicked; she opened the door and versed.

She'd been asking after her brother around the edges of the abyss. She'd approach anybody she heard speaking latin tongue, give a verbal portrait of her brother, imitate his singsong accent, mention his favorite colors, repeat the story of the land he was there to claim, state his place of birth, list all the things he could do, beg them, please, to try to remember if they'd ever come across him. Until the frigid squall forced her to duck into an ATM booth, where she curled up like a dog and after much bone-trembling managed to fall asleep and dreamed that she was scaling one, two, three, seven hills, and when she made it to the top of the eighth she was awakened by the thunderous contempt of the redhead.

It hadn't fully dawned yet – the sky was barely a reddish exhalation that hadn't quite made up its mind to spread over the earth – but by this time the people who might have information for her were already back in the hustle and bustle. She began to walk, rubbing her palms red and pricking up her ears. As she passed the back alley of a restaurant she heard not only a familiar lilt but a voice she knew. She peeked in and saw the youngster from the bus dragging metal cans up beside the restaurant door; he was working energetically, whistling a song from another time, and though he wore only pants and a t-shirt he didn't seem to mind the early-morning chill. He had a small bandage on the hand that Makina had schooled. He smiled on seeing her and made his way over, but as he got closer his face clouded, more with sadness than with fear. I must look terrible, she thought.

Fell on your feet, huh? said Makina.

Damn straight, the boy responded. How bout you?

Ok, but I'm not there yet; there's still someone I have to find.

Your kin came for a grind, too?

74

Yeah, but I don't know where.

The kid pondered for a moment and then said Come with me.

They walked into the restaurant. Makina followed him past rows of cauldrons boiling on the stove, knives, hatchets, cressets, skillets, brokeneck chickens and flopping fish, to a corner where there was a woman deveining a pile of red peppers. She was pale and thin and had an extremely sweet face, but to Makina she looked like Cora, perhaps because of the way she worked, as if undressing her grandchildren for the shower, or because straight away, like with Cora, she felt she could trust her. The woman raised her eyes, fixed them for a second on Makina without ceasing her work on the chiles, and lowered them once more.

Doña, I'm bringing you this girl here, the youngster said. She's looking for one of her kin, and since you seen so many folks come through . . .

Yes, I know, the woman said, but made no attempt to fill the silence that followed.

What? asked Makina. What do you know, señora?

I know who you are.

Did you ever meet my brother?

The woman nodded.

Turned up all sickly and scared as a stray dog, she said. We gave him soup and a sweater and let him sleep under the dish cabinet. Bout a year ago it was, maybe less. Round about that time an anglo woman came, seemed so sad, asking if we didn't have a young man, said she needed one urgent for a job, she seemed like a good person and just so sad, and I told your kin he should go see if that would work for him, cause like I say she looked like a good person but real real mournful and I had no way to know what it was she needed. Your brother went to see her and never came back. Reckon it worked out for him.

And do you know where he went?

Let the boy here take you; I showed him the barrio.

The woman gave the youngster an address and Makina was already rushing him out to the street when she stopped and looked back to ask How did you know who I was? Did my brother tell you how to recognize me?

That too, yes. Told me he had a sister who just by looking at her you could tell she was smart and schooled, said the woman. Yes, that too.

After half a block the youngster was already lagging and decided to give Makina the address of the house where her brother had gone. Makina flew; she literally felt her feet not touching the ground, as if she could float, scissoring her legs till she found her brother and brought him home without setting foot on foreign soil again.

The house was beautiful and big and pink and a wooden fence surrounded it. Makina opened the little gate in the middle of the fence, went up to the front door, rang the bell, waited. She heard a man's footsteps approach and got her hopes up that it was him, that he himself would be the one to open the door, that they'd be reunited right then, no more delays. The door opened and there stood a small man with glasses, wrapped in a purple bathrobe. He was black. Never in her life had she seen so many black people up close, and all of a sudden they seemed to be the key to her quest. Makina glared as though reproaching him for being skinnier and blacker and older than her brother, as though this man were attempting to pass for the other. She was about to say something when he beat her to it with I could put on a blond wig if you like.

Makina was thrown for a second and then laughed, embarrassed.

Sorry, she said in anglo, it's just that I was expecting someone else to open the door.

Someone white? Do you think this is a white person's house?

No, no . . .

Well, right you are, this is a white person's house, there's not a thing I can do about it, except dress like a white person. Do you like my robe?

No . . . Yes . . . I mean, it's just I was expecting someone different.

A different black man? Are you saying I'm not black enough?

Makina laughed. The man laughed. Suddenly her anxiety had passed. For the first time since she'd crossed she felt welcome, even if she still wasn't invited in.

No, not white or black, I'm looking for my brother. They told me he came here to work, in this house.

Oh shoot, the man said with exaggerated disappointment, I knew my prayers couldn't have been answered with such celerity . . . Last night I knelt down and begged the Lord: Lord, send me a woman to relieve me of my misery.

I'm sorry . . .

Right, I know, the brother. He's not here. I'm here. The family that lived here moved. To another continent. They sold the house and I bought it. I don't know why they left, but times are changing and this is a lovely place to stay put.

Makina felt all of the strength she'd been recovering from her own ashes begin to ebb, felt herself extinguishing, felt she wouldn't be able to verse from this one last dead end and that her luck had finally run out. To hell with it all, she thought, to hell with this guy and that one, to hell with all this shit, I'm going to hang myself from a lamppost and let the wind whip me around like an old rag; I'm going to start crying and then I'm going to go to hell too. She gestured farewell to the black man and prepared to go.

There's one left, though, he said.

Makina stared intently, as if trying to read his lips. What?

They left the oldest son behind. He's a soldier. If you go to the army base you'll find him there.

Makina had no idea what so-called respectable people were referring to when they talked about Family. She'd known families that were truncated, extended, bitter, friendly, guileful, doleful, hospitable, ambitious, but never had she known a Happy Family of the sort people talked about, the sort so many swore to defend; all of them were more than just one thing, or they were all the same thing but in completely different ways: none were only fun-loving or solely stingy, and the stories that made any two laugh had nothing in common.

She'd seen people who'd run off to save their families and others who'd run off to be saved from them. Families full of endless table chat as easygoing as families that loved each other without words. (In hers there were just three women right now. Her heart skipped a beat when she thought of her little sister; it only started back up when she concluded that, like her, she'd know how to take care of herself.)

Plus, all families had started off in some mysterious way: to repopulate the earth, or by accident, or by force, or out of boredom; and it's all a mystery what each will become. One time she'd been in the middle of an argument between sweethearts. The woman had run to the switchboard, planted herself behind Makina and stood there responding to each of the man's grievances; it was sheer pigheadedness till Makina began to rephrase their respective complaints: You like my cousin better, you can keep her, She says that was low, you getting with her cousin, What are you bitching about? I'm the same cat I was when you met me, He says he's acting like the man you wanted him to be, Oh, then me too, so don't get in my face cause I already knew that friend of yours, She says what's good for the gander is good for the goose, But you'd never done nothing with him before and me and your cousin was an item, He says that's apples and oranges, I don't care if you was an item back in the day, but I damn sure care if you still are, She says to stop playing dumb, It was just one kiss, the last one, He says they were saying goodbye, Oh, right, then mine was a goodbye, too, She says why can't she if you're still messing around, I'm not saying you can't, but it bugged me when everyone found out, He says he's not that jealous but you shouldn't be so brazen. Then they both shut up and Makina concluded I think you're both saying that the both of you could be more discreet. For a while after that, every time she bumped into them they'd thank her for getting them back together. Then she didn't see them anymore.

On her way to the army base Makina passed a building whose steps were crowded with people holding multicolored flags; her excitement and hurry having subsided, she stopped to see what it was about. There were couples holding hands lining up to see a very solemn man who said something to them and after he said it everyone cried and there was rice and clapping and rejoicing galore. They were getting married. Makina was so dazzled by the beauty of the ceremony that she didn't at first notice that the couples were either men or women but not men and women, and on realizing it she felt moved by how many tears were being shed, like flowers from their eyes, over how hard it had been to get there, and she wished that the people she'd known in the same situation could have been that happy. What she couldn't understand was why the ring, the official, the godparents mattered so. Makina had admired the nerve of her friends who were that way inclined, compared to the tedious smugness of so-called normal marriages; she'd conveyed secret messages, lent her home for the loving that could not speak its name and her clothes for liberation parades. She'd witnessed other ways to love . . . and now they were acting just the same. She felt slightly let down but then said to herself, what did she know. It must be, she thought, that they know other marriages, good ones where people don't split up, where fathers don't leave and they each keep speaking to the other. That must be why they're so happy, and don't mind imitating people who've always despised them. Or perhaps they just want the papers, she said to herself, any kind of papers, even if it's only to fit in; maybe being different gets old after a while.

She went on her way, toward the west, and after many blocks made out another array of flags, equally pretty but all lined up and all the same size. This was where the soldiers were.

7

THE PLACE WHERE PEOPLE'S HEARTS ARE EATEN

Wait here, the soldier said.

As she waited at the entry booth for the anglo whose name the black man had given her, Makina wondered what she'd do if they brought bad news, if they told her that her brother had died or that they had no clue where he might be. Mr. Aitch might lend a hand in exchange for an additional favor, but that would mean mixing with crooks again just for the sake of a tip-off she couldn't necessarily count on. And what was the point of calling the cops when your measure of good fortune consisted of having them not know you exist.

The soldier returned to the booth and sat down behind his desk. He opened a folder and went back to concentrating on the papers he'd been reading before Makina arrived. He'd only just started when he seemed to remember she was there. He looked up and told her the soldier would be with her right away, and went back to his reading.

A few minutes later the door opened and there appeared before her, dressed in military uniform, her very own brother.

Neither one at first recognized the specter of the other. In fact, Makina stood up, greeted him and began to express her gratitude and ask a question before picking up on the soldier's uncanny resemblance to her brother and the unmistakable way in which they differed; he had the same sloping forehead and stiff hair, but looked hardier, and more washed-out. In that fraction of a second she realized her mistake, and that this was her brother, but also that that didn't undo the mistake. She stopped breathing for a second, placed the fingertips of one hand on the desk so as not to lose her balance, and reached out the other to touch the apparition that was this man she had not asked to see. He took her arm, said to the other soldier I'll be right back and versed out to the street with Makina.

They walked awhile in silence. They turned their heads to look at one another, first him, now her, then stared ahead again, disbelieving. They pondered some more what each should say. Finally, still staring straight ahead, he started off:

Did you have a hard time finding me?

Kind of; I only found you when I stopped trying.

How's Cora?

Alive, said Makina; she thought of the message she'd brought him but instead she said What about the land?

Her brother chuckled. You went to see it, didn't you?

Makina nodded.

After that I bounced from back alley to back alley and ass-kicking to ass-kicking, till I met the old lady at the restaurant. She fed me soup till I had strength enough to come home.

But you didn't come home.

No, he said, I didn't come home.

Her brother told Makina an incredible story. After the land fiasco he was too ashamed to return, which is why he accepted the first job that came his way. That woman had come offering the earth itself for his assistance. She spoke latin tongue and asked for his help with every term of entreaty she could find in the dictionary. She took him to her house, introduced him to her husband, to her young daughter, and, after waiting for him to come out of his room, to a bad-tempered teen.

This is who you're going to help, said the woman. But I wanted you to meet the whole family you'll be saving.

He must have been about the same age as him, just barely grown-up. Like him, without consulting his family he'd decided to do something to prove his worth as a man and had joined the army, and in a few days they were going to send him to the other side of the world to fight against who knew what people that had who knew what horrific ways of killing. He was of age, but acted like a child: for the whole insane hour that their interview went on he kept clenching his fists and pursing his lips and only looked up when everything was settled. Over the following days he approached Makina's brother several times to ask who he was, where he came from, if he was scared; but he didn't speak enough of their tongue to respond and only said the name of his Village or the term for its inhabitants, which didn't begin to explain his previous life, or he simply said no, he wasn't scared. The other adolescent nodded and went off tight-lipped, as if there were something he had to say but didn't dare.

This was the deal: Makina's brother would pass himself off as the other. On his return, the family would pay him a sum of money. A large sum, they specified. Plus, he could keep the kid's papers, his name, and his numbers. If he didn't make it back, they'd send the money to his family. And you, would they send you back, too? Makina asked. We didn't discuss that, he replied.

He accepted without quibbling. He was going off with the most powerful army in the world and he thought that was enough of a guarantee that he'd make it back in one piece. He spent his last days before he shipped out at the family's house. They made him learn by heart the answers he'd have to give when he reported, they taught him to copy the signature of the kid he was replacing, he memorized his social security number, they gave him pancakes and warm milk, he was treated well. All those nights he slept in the boy's room and wondered why anyone would give up such a soft bed, but he answered his own question immediately: everyone had to do something for themselves.

The morning he turned up at the barracks he felt an unspeakable fear from the moment he opened his eyes and remembered that that was the day he was going off to war, but he was aware that there was no turning back and he announced himself and answered the questions they asked and signed with the signature he'd learned. The officers who received him looked doubtful at the discrepancy between his name and his face, between his fear and the fact that he'd volunteered, but they took him all the same. And off he went to war.

What was it like? Makina asked. The war.

Her brother tried to avoid the question with a shrug of his shoulders, but the gesture itself betrayed him: when his shoulders returned to their place it was as if they were dragging his whole body down and his expression hardened from the inside out.

Why do you want to know, he said. You wouldn't understand.

So I can understand you.

He took a breath, suddenly raised a hand and tugged Makina's hair; he lowered it again, rubbed it with his other hand and nodded.

It's not like in the movies, he said. I know that here everything seems like in the movies, but it's not like that there. You spend days and days shut in and it's like nothing's going on at all and then one day you go out but you don't know who you're fighting or where you're going to find them. And suddenly you hear your homie died that morning and no one saw where the bullet came from, or you come across a bomb nobody saw get thrown, but there it was, waiting for you. So you gotta go look for them. But when you find them they're not doing jack and you just gotta believe it was them, they were the ones, otherwise you go nuts.

Did you get hurt? Makina asked.

He shook his head and pooched out his lips, neither proud nor relieved.

Not a scratch, he said. So happened that whenever things kicked off I was taking guys out, not getting took . . . Some get a taste for it right away. Not me. Still, you know: if tears are gonna fall, better their house than mine . . .

After he finished his few months' stint he returned to the family's house. He didn't ask them for anything, just went, knocked on the door and got let in. They stared at him with eyes like saucers, astonished to see him there, alive and decorated: alive. He saw it made them uneasy to have him back, as if he were a stranger who'd shown up to talk about something that bore no relation to their white dishes and their white sheets and their station wagon. The father congratulated him, offered him a beer, thanked him on behalf of his country and then began to stammer something about how hard it was to get the money together and how complicated it would be for Makina's brother to use his son's identity and about the possibility of him working for them instead and that way, if he wanted, he could stay in the country legally. But the mother didn't let him finish. Said No. Said We're going to keep our promise. But everyone here knows him, said the father, referring to his offspring. Then we'll go someplace else, the mother replied. We'll change our name, reinvent ourselves, the mother replied.

Since they'd assumed he wasn't coming back, they didn't have the money they'd promised; they gave him something, less than he was hoping for but much more than he could have earned bussing or waiting tables in that time. And they went away.

They bumped into a soldier who started talking to Makina's brother.

Last night I will go to the bar they will tell us about, he said in anglo.

Oh, yeah? How was it, angloed her brother in return.

There will be many women, they will be so pretty, and they will all like the uniform.

Is that so? You speak to any?

Yes, I will speak, I will speak all night, she will give me her number, I will kiss her a little.

First base, huh? Good for you!

I will get very drunk after that. She will go but she will promise that we will see each other again.

Makina's brother laughed and slapped the guy's back, and he carried on his way to the barracks gate.

What was that about? asked Makina.

He's homegrown, he said. Joined up just like me, but still doesn't speak the lingo. Whereas me, I learned it, so every time we see each other he wants to practice. He speaks all one day in past tense, all one day in present, all one day in future, so he can learn his verbs. Today was the future.

And there he was. It was an incredible story, but there was her brother in his battle-worn uniform, alive and in one piece. All of a sudden he had money and a new name, but no clue what to do, where to go, what the path of the person with that name should be.

There wasn't any land to claim. Course you already know that, he said. So I was left hanging.

He stopped and reflected for a minute.

I guess that's what happens to everybody who comes, he continued. We forget what we came for, but there's this reflex to act like we still have some secret plan.

Why not leave, then?

Not now. Too late. I already fought for these people. There must be something they fight so hard for. So I'm staying in the army while I figure out what it is.

But won't they just send you back over there?

He held up his palms. Who knows, we'll see.

They'd made their way back to the entrance to the barracks. They stood there, in silence, until he said I got to go.

Makina nodded. She didn't know what else to say.

You have enough to get back? he asked, anxious. He pulled out his wallet, took out a few bills and handed them to her. Makina accepted them mechanically.

I got to go, he repeated.

He leaned in toward her, and as he gave her a hug said Give Cora a kiss from me. He said it the same way he gave her the hug, like it wasn't his sister he was hugging, like it wasn't his mother he was sending a kiss to, but just a polite platitude. Like he was ripping out her heart, like he was cleanly extracting it and placing it in a plastic bag and storing it in the fridge to eat later.

Sure, said Makina. I'll tell her.

Her brother looked at her one last time, as if from a long way away, turned and walked into the barracks. Makina stood staring at the entrance for some time. Then she pulled out the envelope that Cora had given her, took out the sheet of paper it contained and read it.

Come on back now, it said in Cora's crooked writing. Come on back now, we don't expect anything from you.

/

8

THE SNAKE THAT LIES IN WAIT

She'd already left the barracks when she heard You too! Assume the position! You too! She turned and saw a horribly pasty policeman pointing at her. Are you deaf? Get in line.

In a vacant lot pooled with black water were half a dozen men on their knees, staring at the ground. They all were or looked homegrown. Makina took her place beside them.

You think you can just come here and put your feet up without earning it, said the cop. Well I got news for you: patriots like me are on the lookout and we're going to teach you some manners. Lesson one: get used to falling in. You want to come here, fall in and ask permission, you want to go to the doctor, fall in and ask permission, you want to say a fucking word to me, fall in and ask permission. Fall in and ask permission. Civilized, that's the way we do things around here! We don't jump fences and we don't dig tunnels.

Out the corner of her eye Makina could see the cop's tongue poking out as he talked, all pink and pointy. She could see, too, that even though he didn't draw, he also didn't take his hand off the holster where his gun was. Suddenly the cop addressed one of the others, the one beside her.

What you got there?

He took two steps toward him and repeated What you got there?

The man was holding a little book and gripped it tighter when the cop came close. He resisted a bit but finally let him snatch it away.

Ha, said the cop after glancing at it. Poetry. Lookie here at the educated worker, comes with no money, no papers, but hey, poems. You a romantic? A poet? A writer? Looks like we're going to find out.

He ripped out one of the last pages, laid it on the book's cover, pulled a pencil from his shirt and gave it all to the man.

Write.

The man looked up, bewildered.

I told you to write, not look at me, you piece of shit. Keep your eyes on the paper and write why you think you're up the creek, why you think your ass is in the hands of this patriotic officer. Or don't you know what you did wrong? Sure you do. Write.

The man pressed the pencil to the paper and began

to trace a letter but his trembling prevented him. He dropped the pencil, picked it up, and tried again. He couldn't compose a single word, just nervous scribble.

Makina suddenly snatched the pencil and book away. The cop roared I didn't tell you to . . . But he fell silent on seeing that Makina had begun to write with determination. He kept a close watch on her progress, smiling and sardonic the whole time, though he was disconcerted and couldn't hide it.

Makina wrote without stopping to think which word was better than which other or how the message was turning out. She wrote ten lines and when she was done she placed the pencil on the book and fixed her gaze upon it. The cop waited a few seconds, then said Give me that, took the sheet of paper and began to read aloud:

We are to blame for this destruction, we who don't speak your tongue and don't know how to keep quiet either. We who didn't come by boat, who dirty up your doorsteps with our dust, who break your barbed wire. We who came to take your jobs, who dream of wiping your shit, who long to work all hours. We who fill your shiny clean streets with the smell of food, who brought you violence you'd never known, who deliver your dope, who deserve to be chained by neck and feet. We who are happy to die for you, what else could we do? We, the ones who are waiting for who knows what.

We, the dark, the short, the greasy, the shifty, the fat, the anemic. We the barbarians.

The cop had started off in a mock-portentous voice but gradually abandoned the histrionics as he neared the last line, which he read almost in a whisper. After that he went on staring at the paper as if he'd gotten stuck on the final period. When he finally looked up, his rage, or his interest in his captives, seemed to have dissolved. He crumpled the paper into a ball and tossed it behind him. Then he looked away, turned his back, spoke over the radio to someone and took off.

Makina stood as soon as the cop had gone, but the others took some time to realize they weren't under arrest. They looked at one another, half glad and half mistrustful, then looked at Makina but couldn't say anything to her because she'd started walking again and all they could make out was her silhouette against the sun.

9

THE OBSIDIAN PLACE WITH NO WINDOWS OR HOLES FOR THE SMOKE

She couldn't stop, she had to keep walking even if she didn't know how she was going to get back. It was the rhythm, it was her burden-free body, it was the soft sound of her own panting that pushed her on. She quickened her step; with the ashen sun head-on she walked down gray streets and past houses that were all the same, like little boxes lined up in a storefront window.

She came to a park all atwitter with birds about to go to sleep. She walked straight through the middle of it, not around it on the sidewalk, and with each step her feet – pad, pad, pad – left an imprint on the earth. The evening clouded over until you couldn't see more than one step ahead, and yet Makina didn't stop: she walked quickly – pad, pad, pad – guiding herself by the trilling in the trees. Suddenly she heard Watch how you go, darlin.

She turned to see who had spoken, because they'd said it in latin tongue, and saw that there, sitting on a bench looking exactly like himself and also quite different – like varnished over, like meaner, or with a bigger nose – was Chucho, grinning at her. First she saw the ember, then the man who made it glow. Makina felt herself smile though she didn't feel the emotion behind the smile because she'd somehow been emptied of feelings by now.

What are you doing here? she asked.

Doing my thing, looking out for you.

Don't you work for Aitch? Mr. Q is the one who was supposed to help me on this side.

I work for whoever hires me. Never stopped watching you, I know where you been and how tough things got.

Things are tough all over, but here I'm all mixed up, I just don't understand this place.

Don't let it get you down. They don't understand it either, they live in fear of the lights going out, as if every day wasn't already made of lightning and blackouts. They need us. They want to live forever but still can't see that for that to work they need to change color and number. But it's already happening.

Chucho took a drag on his cigarette so deep he almost consumed it all. Then he said And now you're here, follow me. He stood and Makina walked beside him. They left the park, entered a little maze of streets that looked like they belonged to some other city and stopped before a low, narrow door behind which nothing could be seen.

Go on in, Chucho said, pointing.

Here? What is this place?

Here's where they'll give you a hand.

Makina crouched down to fit through the door, and on taking the first step felt a cold wind coming from inside but didn't get cold herself; she saw the top of a spiral staircase. She began to descend, turned to see if Chucho was following but he had stayed at the door, blew her a kiss, moved out of the frame and Makina caught a glimpse of the last rays of sun. Then she went on down. After four spiral turns she came to another door, which was answered by a handsome old woman with very long white fingernails and a powdered face, wearing a butterfly pin that held back the folds of her dress. Over the door was a sign that said *Verse*. She tried to remember how to say verse in any of her tongues but couldn't. This was the only word that came to her lips. Verse. The woman drew two cigarettes from a black case, lit them both and held one out. Makina took it and stepped through.

The place was like a sleepwalker's bedroom: specific yet inexact, somehow unreal and yet vivid; there were lots of people, very calm, all smoking, and though she saw no ventilation shafts nor felt any currents the air didn't smell. Like a song from long ago, a sudden apprehension made her think something terrible was going to occur any second. Something's about to happen, something's about to happen. She tensed and felt she loved her skin, but the tension soon gave way, lulled by the only clear and distinguishable sound in the place. She hadn't noticed it until now: there was no music, no conversation, just the sound of running water, not like through the plumbing but the energetic coursing of subterranean rivers that reminded her that it had been a while since she'd washed, and yet she wasn't dirty, didn't smell bad – didn't smell at all.

What's going to happen, she wondered.

Then, making his way toward her from among the crowd, she saw a tall, thin man draped in a baggy leather jacket. He had protruding teeth that yellowed his enormous smile. He stopped in front of her.

Here. He held out a file. All taken care of.

Makina took the file and looked at its contents. There she was, with another name, another birthplace. Her photo, new numbers, new trade, new home. I've been skinned, she whispered.

When she looked up the man was no longer there and she tipped briefly into panic, she felt for a second – or for many seconds; she couldn't tell because she didn't have a watch, nobody had a watch – that the turmoil of so many new things crowding in on the old ones was more than she could take; but a second – or many – later she stopped feeling the weight of uncertainty and guilt; she thought back to her people as though recalling the contours of a lovely landscape that was now fading away: the Village, the Little Town, the Big Chilango, all those colors, and she saw that what was happening was not a cataclysm; she understood with all of her body and all of her memory, she truly understood, and when everything in the world fell silent finally said to herself I'm ready.

TRANSLATOR'S NOTE

There could hardly be a more appropriate time for the English publication of Yuri Herrera's *Signs Preceding the End of the World*. For, in its nine short chapters, this remarkable novel explores not only the timeless themes of epic journey, death, and the underworld, but also many of the pressing issues of our times: migration, immigration (and two of its stomach-churning corollaries, so-called nativism and profiling), transnationalism, transculturalism, and language hybridity – not to mention, of course, the end of the world.

How, then, to recreate all of this in English? Undertaking a translation requires first determining what makes the text in question so striking, and, in the case of *Signs*, that turns out to be quite a long list. In the same way that the novel delves into a large number of themes within a very short space, Yuri Herrera's prose, too, exhibits a multitude of distinct characteristics, displaying great variations in what is always creative and often non-standard language: its rhythm and orality; a style that is elegantly spare; striking metaphors, which are often unusual but rarely jarring; a mix of registers both low and high – slang and colloquial but also lyrical and eloquent, some rural and others urban and both often very Mexican (or very much of its border); and neologism, to name just some. There is also the overall tone, which is intimate and often infused with understated affection and tenderness. And there is the fact that all of this manages to sound entirely natural. Yuri Herrera's use of language is nothing short of stunning, and translating it is both fulfilling and daunting; what makes his writing so unique is what makes it so challenging to translate.

To prepare for the project, as many translators do, I first read widely. I read for theme; I read for tone; I read for style. I read texts that took place on borders. I read about Aztec mythology and *Alice in Wonderland* and Dante's circles of hell. I tried to read writers who might have styles, or tones, or non-standard usage that I would find in some way comparable or analogous. The most helpful was Cormac McCarthy (in particular *The Road*, another tale – coincidentally, or not? – that can be read on different levels, one of which is "the end of the world"). I made word lists and devised ways to be non-standard in English (unusual collocations, creative compound nouns, nominalization of verbs and verbalization of nouns). I looked for ways to work in alliteration to lend the English rhythm, to lend it sonority. And even if much of this was culled during successive revisions and edits, these strategies informed the entire undertaking of the project, leaving their mark.

In addition, I tried to create an English that was geographically non-explicit, although, like me, the translation speaks mostly American English. To explain what I mean by that, let me offer a couple of examples. The novel's dialogues are often peppered with language – colloquialisms, slang, expressions, culturally-embedded references – that could only take place in Mexico (or on the Mexico–USA border). Translating only what readers might see as the *meaning* of these conversations and references might arguably produce a comprehensible and accurate text, though it would lose its regional flavor and intimacy (think of the difference between "a bonnie lass" and "a pretty girl," for instance). Nevertheless, attempting to find an English dialect that would serve as a linguistic "parallel" is problematic. Should Mexican gangsters speak like mobsters in *The Godfather*? If not, is there another group they should speak like? My answer is "no." Instead, I've endeavored to do two things. First, I have sometimes "marked" the language as non-standard in ways that are not geographically recognizable. In dialogues, this meant emphasizing the oral nature of the language (using colloquialisms such as "yond" for "over there," abbreviating "about" to "bout," for example). Second, I have occasionally left specific words in Spanish, deliberately choosing not to translate. When a character calls his mother *jefecita*, for example (literally, "little boss" – a not terribly uncommon term of endearment), she remains *jefecita* in the translation. My intention here is to leave a linguistic reminder to the reader that this is, in fact, a translated text, and to avoid renderings ("momma," "moms," etc.) that might be genuinely intimate, but cringe-makingly American for language meant to come out of a rural Mexican teenager's mouth.

Unsurprisingly, I also spent a tremendous amount of time considering possibilities for the novel's most talked-about neologism: *jarchar*. Yuri himself has discussed this verb in multiple places. Within *Signs*, it means, essentially, "to leave." The word is derived from *jarchas* (from the Arabic *kharja*, meaning exit), which were short Mozarabic verses or couplets tacked on to the end of longer Arabic or Hebrew poems written in Al-Andalus, the region we now call Spain. Written in the vernacular, these lyric compositions served as a sort of bridge between cultures and languages, Mozarabic being a kind of hybrid that was, of course, not yet Spanish. And on one level *Signs* is just that: a book about bridging cultures and languages. *Jarchar*, too, is a noun-turned-verb. I wrangled with myself – and spoke somewhat obsessively with others – over how best to render this term, debating multiple options before finally deciding on "to verse" (the two runners-up were "to port" and "to twain"). Used in context it is easily understood, and has the added benefits of also being a noun-turned-verb, a term clearly referring to poetry, and part of several verbs involving motion and communication (traverse, reverse, converse) as well as the "end" of the uni-verse. Makina, the protagonist, is the character who most often "verses," as well as the woman who serves as a bridge between cultures, languages and worlds. Would readers realize any of this had it not just been explained? I doubt it. But that's ok; the same is true of the Spanish. Opening with a sinkhole large enough to kill people and closing with another subterranean sequence, the book takes us full circle in a variety of ways.

This translation has benefited from the direct and indirect input of many people whom I'd like to thank. It was Katherine Silver who initially sent the opportunity to translate Yuri my way. I also gained from the encouragement, suggestions, edits, discussions, pep talks, emails, readings, and other forms of support of friends, mentors, and editors including Peter Bush, Jean Dangler, Lorna Scott Fox, Daniel Hahn, Henry Reese, Samantha Schnee, and Lawrence Venuti. I would like especially to thank Drew Whitelegg for multiple re-readings, endless discussions and encouragement.

And my absolute deepest thanks go to Yuri himself, for answering hundreds of emails (often many per day, sometimes with a dozen questions each) as well as generously discussing in person some of the novel's many nuances, providing constant encouragement and always being open to exploring new avenues of interpretation.

Lisa Dillman
Decatur, Georgia, USA
February 2014

Dear readers,

We rely on subscriptions from people like you to tell these other stories – the types of stories most publishers consider too risky to take on.

Our subscribers don't just make the books physically happen. They also help us approach booksellers, because we can demonstrate that our books already have readers and fans. And they give us the security to publish in line with our values, which are collaborative, imaginative and "shamelessly literary."

All of our subscribers:

- receive a first-edition copy of each of the books they subscribe to
- are thanked by name at the end of these books
- are warmly invited to contribute to our plans and choice of future books

BECOME A SUBSCRIBER, OR GIVE A SUBSCRIPTION TO A FRIEND

Visit andotherstories.org/subscribe to become part of an alternative approach to publishing.

Subscriptions are:

£20 for two books per year

£35 for four books per year

£50 for six books per year

OTHER WAYS TO GET INVOLVED

If you'd like to know about upcoming events and reading groups (our foreign-language reading groups help us choose books to publish, for example) you can:

- join the mailing list at: andotherstories.org/join-us
- follow us on Twitter: @andothertweets
- join us on Facebook: facebook.com/AndOtherStoriesBooks
- follow our blog: Ampersand

This book was made possible thanks to the support of:

Abigail Miller
Adam Lenson
Adrian May
Aidan
   Cottrell-Boyce
Ajay Sharma
Alan Cameron
Alan Ramsey
Alannah Hopkin
Alasdair Hutchison
Alasdair Thomson
Alastair Dickson
Alastair Gillespie
Alec Begley
Alex Martin
Alex Ramsey
Alexander Balk
Alexandra Buchler
Alexandra de
   Scitivaux
Alexandra de
   Verseg-Roesch
Ali Conway
Ali Smith
Alice Brett
Alice Nightingale
Alice Toulmin
Alison Bowyer
Alison Hughes
Alison Layland

Allison Graham
Alyse Ceirante
Amanda Anderson
Amanda Dalton
Amanda Jane
   Stratton
Amanda Love
   Darragh
Amber Dowell
Amelia Ashton
Amy Capelin
Amy McDonnell
Ana Amália Alves
Andrea Davis
Andrew Marston
Andrew McCafferty
Andrew Nairn
Andrew Whitelegg
Andy Burfield
Andy Chick
Angela Creed
Angela Thirlwell
Ann McAllister
Ann Van Dyck
Anna Britten
Anna Demming
Anna Holmwood
Anna Milsom
Anna Vinegrad
Anna-Maria Aurich

Annabel Hagg
Annalise Pippard
Anne Carus
Anne Marie Jackson
Anne Maguire
Anne Meadows
Anne Waugh
Annie McDermott
Anonymous
Anthony Quinn
Antonio de Swift
Antony Pearce
Aoife Boyd
Archie Davies
Arline Dillman
Asher Norris
Averill Buchanan

Barbara Adair
Barbara Mellor
Barry Hall
Barry Norton
Bartolomiej Tyszka
Belinda Farrell
Ben Schofield
Ben Smith
Ben Thornton
Benjamin Judge
Benjamin Morris
Bettina Debon

Bianca Jackson
Blanka Stoltz
Bob Richmond-
    Watson
Brenda Scott
Brendan McIntyre
Briallen Hopper
Brigita Ptackova
Bruce Ackers
Bruce & Maggie
    Holmes
Bruce Millar

C Baker
C Mieville
Candy Says Juju
    Sophie
Carl Emery
Caroline
    Maldonado
Caroline
    Mildenhall
Caroline Perry
Carolyn A
    Schroeder
Catherine Taylor
Cecilia Rossi
Cecily Maude
Charles Beckett
Charles
    Fernyhough
Charles Lambert

Charles Rowley
Charlotte Holtam
Charlotte
    Middleton
Charlotte Ryland
Charlotte Whittle
Chris Day
Chris Elcock
Chris Gribble
Chris Hancox
Chris Lintott
Chris Stevenson
Chris Watson
Chris Wood
Christina Baum
Christine Luker
Christopher Allen
Christopher
    Marlow
Christopher Terry
Ciara Ní Riain
Ciarán Oman
Claire C Riley
Claire Mitchell
Claire Tranah
Clarissa Botsford
Clifford Posner
Clive Bellingham
Colin Burrow
Collette Eales
Courtney Lilly

Damien Tuffnell
Dan Pope
Daniel Arnold
Daniel Barley
Daniel Carpenter
Daniel Gallimore
Daniel Gillespie
Daniel Hahn
Daniel Hugill
Daniel Lipscombe
Daniel Venn
Daniela
    Steierberg
Dave Lander
David Archer
David Eales
David Craig Hall
David Hedges
David
    Johnson-Davies
David Jones
David Roberts
David Smith
David Wardrop
Deborah Bygrave
Deborah Jacob
Deborah Smith
Delia Cowley
Denis Stillewagt &
    Anca Fronescu
Diana Brighouse
Diana Fox Carney

Dimitris Melicertes

Dominique Brocard

E Jarnes

Ed Tallent

Eddie Dick

Eileen Buttle

Elaine Rassaby

Eleanor Maier

Eliza O'Toole

Elizabeth Cochrane

Elizabeth Costello

Elizabeth Draper

Emily Diamand

Emily Jeremiah

Emily Yaewon
    Lee & Gregory
    Limpens

Emily Rhodes

Emily Taylor

Emily Williams

Emma Bielecki

Emma Kenneally

Emma Teale

Emma Timpany

Eric Langley

Erin Louttit

Eva Tobler-
    Zumstein

Evgenia Loginova

Ewan Tant

Fawzia Kane

Federay Holmes

Fi McMillan

Fiona Graham

Fiona Malby

Fiona Marquis

Fiona Powlett
    Smith

Fiona Quinn

Fran Carter

Fran Sanderson

Frances
    Chapman

Francis Taylor

Francisco Vilhena

Freya Carr

Friederike Knabe

G Thrower

Gale Pryor

Gavin Collins

Gawain Espley

Genevra
    Richardson

Geoffrey Cohen

Geoffrey Fletcher

George McCaig

George Sandison &
    Daniela Laterza

George Savona

George Wilkinson

Georgia Panteli

Gill Boag-Munroe

Gillian Jondorf

Gillian Stern

Gina Dark

Glyn Ridgley

Gordon Cameron

Gordon Campbell

Gordon
    Mackechnie

Grace Dyrness

Graham R Foster

Graham & Steph
    Parslow

Guy Haslam

Hannah Ellis

Hannah Perret

Hanne Larsson

Hannes Heise

Harriet Mossop

Harriet Owles

Harriet Spencer

Helen Asquith

Helen Buck

Helen Collins

Helen Weir

Helen Wormald

Helena Taylor

Helene Walters

Henrike
    Laehnemann

Henry Hitchings

Holly Johnson &
    Pat Merloe
Howdy Reisdorf

Ian Barnett
Ian McMillan
Inna Carson
Irene Mansfield
Isobel Dixon
Isobel Staniland

J Collins
JP Sanders
Jack Brown
Jack Browne
Jacqueline Crooks
Jacqueline Haskell
Jacqueline
    Lademann
Jacqueline Taylor
Jacquie Goacher
Jade Maitre
Jade Yap
James Cubbon
James Huddie
James Portlock
James Scudamore
James Tierney
James Upton
Jane Brandon
Jane Whiteley
Jane Woollard

Janet Mullarney
Janette Ryan
Jason Spencer
Jeff Collins
Jen Grainger
Jen
    Hamilton-Emery
Jennifer Campbell
Jennifer Higgins
Jennifer Hurstfield
Jennifer O'Brien
Jennifer Stobart
Jennifer Watson
Jenny Diski
Jenny Newton
Jeremy Weinstock
Jeremy Wood
Jerry Lynch
Jess Wood
Jessica Kingsley
Jim Boucherat
Jo Elvery
Jo Harding
Jo Hope
Joanna Ellis
Joanna Neville
Joe Gill
Joe Robins
Joel Love
Johan Forsell
Johannes Georg Zipp
John Conway

John Fisher
John Gent
John Griffiths
John Hodgson
John Kelly
John McGill
John Nicholson
John Stephen
    Grainger
Jon Gower
Jon Iglesias
Jon Lindsay Miles
Jon Riches
Jonathan Evans
Jonathan Ruppin
Jonathan Watkiss
Joseph Cooney
Joshua Davis
Judy Kendall
Julia Sutton
Julian Duplain
Julian Lomas
Juliane Jarke
Julie Freeborn
Julie Gibson
Julie Van Pelt
Juliet Swann
Juraj Janik

KL Ee
Kaarina Hollo
Kaitlin Olson

Kapka Kassabova
Karan Deep Singh
Kari Dickson
Karla Fonseca
Katarina Trodden
Kate Beswick
Kate Gardner
Kate Griffin
Kate Pullinger
Kate Wild
Kate Young
Katharina Liehr
Katharine Freeman
Katharine Robbins
Katherine El-Salahi
Katherine Jacomb
Katherine Wootton
   Joyce
Kathryn Lewis
Katia Leloutre
Katie Brown
Katie Martin
Kay Elmy
Keith Alldritt
Keith Dunnett
Keith Walker
Kevin Acott
Kevin Brockmeier
Kevin Pino
Kinga Burger
Koen Van Bockstal
Kristin Djuve

Krystalli
   Glyniadakis

Lana Selby
Lander Hawes
Larry Colbeck
Lauren Cerand
Lauren Ellemore
Leanne Bass
Leeanne O'Neill
Leigh Vorhies
Leonie Schwab
Lesley Lawn
Lesley Watters
Leslie Rose
Linda Broadbent
Lindsay Brammer
Lindsey Ford
Lindsey Stuart
Liz Clifford
Liz Ketch
Liz Tunnicliffe
Liz Wilding
Loretta Platts
Lorna Bleach
Louise S Smith
Louise Bongiovanni
Louise Rogers
Lucy Caldwell
Luke Healey
Luke Williams
Lynn Martin

M Manfre
Maeve Lambe
Maggie Humm
Maggie Livesey
Maggie Peel
Maisie & Nick
   Carter
Malcolm Bourne
Mandy Boles
Marella
   Oppenheim
Margaret E Briggs
Margaret Jull Costa
Marina Castledine
Marina Galanti
Marina Jones
Marion Cole
Mark Ainsbury
Mark Blacklock
Mark Howdle
Mark Lumley
Mark Richards
Mark Stevenson
Mark Waters
Martha Gifford
Martha Nicholson
Martin Brampton
Martin Conneely
Martin Hollywood
Martin Price
Martin Whelton
Mary Hall

Mary Nash

Mary Wang

Mason Billings

Mathias Enard

Matt Oldfield

Matthew Francis

Matthew
    Lawrence

Matthew O'Dwyer

Matthew Smith

Maureen Freely

Maxime
    Dargaud-Fons

Meryl Hicks

Michael Harrison

Michael Johnston

Michelle
    Bailat-Jones

Michelle Roberts

Miles Visman

Milo Waterfield

Mitchell Albert

Monika Olsen

Morgan Lyons

Moshi Moshi
    Records

Murali Menon

Nadine El-Hadi

Naomi Frisby

Naomi Kruger

Nasser Hashmi

Natalie
    Brandweiner

Natalie Smith

Natalie Wardle

Nathan Rostron

Neil Pretty

Nia Emlyn-Jones

Nick Chapman

Nick James

Nick Nelson &
    Rachel Eley

Nick Sidwell

Nicola Balkind

Nicola Cowan

Nicola Hart

Nina Alexandersen

Nina Power

Nuala Watt

Octavia Kingsley

Olga Zilberbourg

Olivia Heal

Owen Booth

PM Goodman

Pamela Ritchie

Pat Crowe

Patricia Appleyard

Patrick Famcombe

Patrick Owen

Paul C Daw

Paul M Cray

Paul Bailey

Paul Brand

Paul Dettman

Paul Gamble

Paul Hannon

Paul Jones

Paul Miller

Paul Myatt

Penelope Price

Peter Burns

Peter Law

Peter Lawton

Peter McCambridge

Peter Murray

Peter Rowland

Peter Vos

Philip Warren

Philippe Royer

Phillip Canning

Phyllis Reeve

Piet Van Bockstal

Piotr Kwiecinski

Polly McLean

Rachel Kennedy

Rachel Lasserson

Rachel Van Riel

Rachel Watkins

Rachael Williams

Read MAW Books

Rebecca Atkinson

Rebecca Braun

Rebecca Carter
Rebecca Moss
Rebecca Rosenthal
Réjane Collard
Richard Dew
Richard Ellis
Richard Jackson
Richard Martin
Richard Smith
Rishi Dastidar
Rob
　Jefferson-Brown
Robert Gillett
Robin Patterson
Robin Woodburn
Rodolfo Barradas
Ros Schwartz
Rose Cole
Rosemary Rodwell
Rosemary Terry
Rosie Pinhorn
Ross Macpherson
Roz Simpson
Rufus Johnstone
Ruth Diver
Ruth Stokes
Ruth Van Driessche

SJ Bradley
Sally Baker
Sam Cunningham
Sam Gallivan

Sam Gordon
Sam Ruddock
Samantha
　Sabbarton-
　Wright
Samantha Sawers
Samantha Schnee
Samuel Alexander
　Mansfield
Sandra de Monte
Sandra Hall
Sara D'Arcy
Sarah Benson
Sarah Bourne
Sarah Butler
Sarah Fakray
Sarah Salmon
Sarah Salway
Sascha Feuchert
Scott Morris
Sean Malone
Sean McGivern
Seini O'Connor
Sergio Gutierrez
　Negron
Sharon Evans
Shaun Whiteside
Sheridan Marshall
Sherine El-Sayed
Shirley Harwood
Sian O'Neill
Sigrun Hodne

Simon Armstrong
Simon John Harvey
Simon Okotie
Simon Pare
Simon Pennington
Simone O'Donovan
Siobhan Higgins
Sioned Puw
　Rowlands
Sonia McLintock
Sophia Wickham
Sophie Johnstone
Sophie North
Stefano D'Orilia
Steph Morris
Stephen H Oakey
Stephen Abbott
Stephen Bass
Stephen Pearsall
Stewart McAbney
Susan Murray
Susan Shriver
Susan Tomaselli
Susanna Jones
Susie Roberson
Suzanne Smith
Suzanne White
Sylvie Zannier-Betts

Tammy Harman
Tammy Watchorn
Tamsin Ballard

Tamsin Walker
Tania Hershman
Tasmin Maitland
The Mighty Douche
    Softball Team
Thees Spreckelsen
Thomas JD Gray
Thomas Bell
Thomas Fritz
Tien Do
Tim Jackson
Tim Theroux
Tim Warren
Timothy Harris
Tina Andrews
Tina Rotherham-
    Winqvist
Tom Bowden

Tom Darby
Tom Franklin
Tony & Joy
    Molyneaux
Torna Russell-Hills
Tracy Northup
Trevor Lewis
Trevor Wald
Trilby Humphryes
Tristan Burke
Troy Zabel

Val Challen
Vanessa Jackson
Vanessa Nolan
Vasco Dones
Victoria Adams
Victoria Walker

Visaly Muthusamy
Vivien
    Doornekamp-
    Glass

Wendy Irvine
Wendy Langridge
Wendy Toole
Wenna Price
William G Dennehy

Yukiko Hiranuma

Zara Todd
Zoe Brasier
Zoë Perry

Current & Upcoming Books

Born in Actopan, Mexico, in 1970, **Yuri Herrera** studied in Mexico and El Paso and took his PhD at Berkeley. *Signs Preceding the End of the World (Señales que precederán al fin del mundo)* was shortlisted for the Rómulo Gallegos Prize and is being published in several languages. And Other Stories will publish his two other novels, starting with *The Transmigration of Bodies* in 2016. Herrera is currently teaching at the University of Tulane in New Orleans.

Lisa Dillman is based in Atlanta, Georgia, where she translates Spanish, Catalan, and Latin American writers, and teaches at Emory University. Her recent translations include *The Frost on His Shoulders* by Lorenzo Mediano, *Op Oloop* by Juan Filloy (longlisted for the Best Translated Book Award), *Me, Who Dove into the Heart of the World* by Sabina Berman, and *Rain Over Madrid* by Andrés Barba. She is obsessed with words, running, cooking, and her dog, Maya.